The Official Mermaid Handbook

Sally Huss

ISBN: 10: 1-945742186
ISBN 13: 9781945742187

One evening, as Maggie, the Mermaid, lay on her bed of lacy seaweed, wrapped in a quilt of giant kelp fronds, she looked over at her fish tank and watched the goldfish swim in and out of it. They were all alike, she thought, just like so many mermaids.

She reached over, turned on her nightlight – a lovely, blue, electric eel…

picked up her journal with its water lily pages and began to write.

The ink in her baby octopus pen seemed a bit slow in flowing.
So she tickled it just enough to get it working properly.

I want to be different, she thought. *I want to be GREAT!* she wrote.

Then she closed her journal, turned off her light and went to sleep.

In the morning, over a bowl of her favorite cereal – crispy wrack flakes with whale milk – she announced to her mother and father: "I want to be GREAT!"

"That's nice, dear," said her mother, knowing that Maggie was one of thousands of mermaids living in the ocean and it was very unlikely that she would be destined to be great or great at anything. They were a regular merfolk family and "great" was something to which none of them aspired.

But mother wished her daughter well and handed her a lunch of pickled sea urchins with red kelp salsa, as Maggie headed out the grotto door on her way to school.

Luckily for Maggie, her favorite dolphin, Henry, was nearby and offered her a ride to school. She would never turn down a ride from Henry because he always took the scenic route through fields of seaweed and over coral hills covered with colorful sea anemones.

When she finally arrived at school and sat down in class, she found herself luckier still. Her teacher, Miss Crandall, announced to the class that the subject for the day was "GREATNESS." Imagine that?

Miss Crandall told her class of mermaids that they each had a special talent and if they would just develop this talent, they could certainly become great!

Miss Crandall explained, "As we all know, Alicia likes to sing, but she might even sing better and become a great singer if she were trained by a professional and practiced very hard for a long time.

Then, there's Sally," said Miss Crandall. "We all know that Sally likes to paint watercolors." Miss Crandall pointed to one of Sally's creations hanging on the wall. "Perhaps if she keeps it up, she will become a great painter.

Lucia likes to dance and Lila toots her conch shell whenever she gets a chance. Who knows how great they can become?" continued Miss Crandall, as she wandered among the mermaids.

Without waiting to be mentioned, Mindy swam to the top of the classroom flagpole, spread her arms wide and did a double flip ending in a swan dive. "Perfect!" exclaimed Miss Crandall. "Perhaps if Mindy keeps it up, one day she may represent us in the Olympics!"

Turning to Maggie, Miss Crandall asked, "What about you, Maggie? What would you like to be?"

Without a moment's hesitation, Maggie blurted out, "I want to be GREAT!"

"Yes, I know," said Miss Crandall. "But great at what?"

Hmmmm. Maggie didn't know. She thought about this for the rest of the day.

On her way home, she stopped at the library, hoping to find some help. Speaking to the librarian, she asked, "I'd like a book about being great. Do you have any books about that?"

"Great at what?" asked the librarian.

"Just great!" Maggie replied.

The librarian thought for a moment, then said, "Well, until you decide what you want to be, how about being great at what you are - - a mermaid? Let's start with that."

She turned to a long shelf of books and pulled one out and handed it to Maggie, saying, "Here's a book about being the best that you can be. If you finish this book and do what it says, you will certainly be **GREAT**!"

Maggie read the title out loud, "The Official Mermaid Handbook." Then she tucked it under her arm. "This will do," she said. And left.

That night after dinner, Maggie opened the book and began to read.

It said: *This handbook is for those mermaids who wish to develop their greatness. In this way they will help make the world — our ocean — a better place. If you are one of these mermaids, read on.*

Maggie was not sure how developing her greatness was going to make the world better, but it sounded interesting and at the same time, exciting. Maggie read on.

Here are the requirements for becoming a great mermaid:

Number 1 – A great mermaid must know how to swim, and swim well.

"Oh, boy," said Maggie, "this is going to be easy." With that she swam a couple of laps around her room just to prove to herself that she was on her way to greatness. After all, she had been swimming all her life.

She put her book away; that was enough for one day.

The next morning before breakfast, she thought she'd take a peek at the next requirement for being great.

Number 2 – A great mermaid always presents herself in a clean and attractive manner (except when she is playing) and also keeps her surroundings orderly.

Maggie looked in the mirror. Her hair was disheveled, her scales were ruffled, and her room was a mess.

Within five minutes, Maggie whirled around her room straightening, fluffing, flattening, and fixing herself and her surroundings, making herself perfectly presentable to King Neptune, king of the sea, if he should swim in.

Number 3 she read on her way to breakfast.

Number 3 — A great mermaid says "Please" and "Thank You" when asking for or receiving anything.

She thought about this as she sat down next to her little brother, a tadpole of a merman, with whom she'd had many arguments.

Today was no different. He had control of the lichen pancakes, a favorite of Maggie's. She reached for the plate, but before she could touch it, he yanked it out of her range. Then, he smiled… she glared.

All of a sudden, she came to her senses. In the sweetest voice she could muster, asked her brother, "Please pass the pancakes." Surprisingly, he did. She smiled and said, "Thank you." Becoming a great mermaid has its perks, she thought.

Requirement number 4 she read on the way to school.

Number 4 – A great mermaid is always kind and helpful.

Surprisingly, an opportunity to be kind and helpful presented itself. The tail of another mermaid had gotten caught in a clamshell. This was not an unusual occurrence, but it was certainly an unpleasant one.

"Here, Sophia," she said. "Hold still. I'll pry it open." And with a trick she had learned from an old hermit crab, she tempted the clam into letting go by offering him a treat from her lunch sack -- a nori cracker with fish eggs on top. He couldn't resist.

"Thank you, Maggie," said Sophia.

"You're welcome," replied Maggie. ("You're welcome" was probably on the great mermaid requirement list somewhere, along with "Please" and "Thank you.")

In class that day, the mermaids' teacher had given them a special project – build a sand castle. They couldn't be more delighted. Each helped in her own way, and Maggie pitched in appropriately without taking over the activities.

She added her special decorative skills by sharing her very own cerith shells and placing them along the castle walls.

"Well done!" they all agreed when it was finished.

Well done it was for Maggie when on the way home she read in her handbook that Number 5 was about cooperation.

Number 5 — A great mermaid works well with others and shares what she has.

Maggie was so delighted with herself that she jumped ahead and read about the next requirement for being great.

Number 6 – A great mermaid is adventurous and tries new things.

Perfect, thought Maggie, tonight's the night.

When she swam through her front door she announced,
"I'm cooking dinner tonight!" Her mother was stunned. Her father
was baffled, and her brother held his nose.

Into the kitchen she went, mixing and stirring, baking and tossing, pouring and flouring until she had an entire meal created.

When the family sat down to dinner, they said grace – giving thanks for what they were about to receive – and hoped for the best.

The food was different but it was delicious – sour fish fingers, turtle soup, brisket of starfish, and soon to be everyone's favorite – salt water caramel ice cream.

Maggie was moving along smartly on her quest to being great, when a stumbling block showed up. It was an accident really but all the same, it proved that she had not reached greatness yet.

It happened on a typical day of school when all of the mermaids were to turn in their homework assignments. As Miss Crandall swam down the aisle picking up the papers, she stopped at Maggie's desk.

Maggie was horrified. Not only had she not brought her homework, she hadn't done it. She had just forgotten.

Miss Crandall looked at her and the only thing Maggie could think to do was to tell a fib. "My pet lobster ate it," she said sheepishly.

Miss Crandall looked at her again and as Maggie stared into her teacher's eyes, she remembered what she read last night in her handbook –

Number 7 – A great mermaid always tells the truth and takes responsibility for her actions.

And –

Number 8 – A great mermaid is courageous.

If not now, thought Maggie, perhaps never. She put it all together and with a great deal of courage said, "I lied. I didn't do my homework. I forgot."

Miss Crandall said, "Thank you for telling the truth. Do two assignments for tomorrow. That will put things right."

"Thank you, Miss Crandall," said Maggie, showing great respect for her teacher and honoring the ninth requirement.

Number 9 – A great mermaid shows respect for authority.

Maggie was rounding the bend on this idea of becoming great when she got home from school and read Number 10.

Number 10 – A great mermaid always maintains a positive attitude.

"What does that mean?" Maggie wanted to know, as she read it to her mother.

"It means that you remain happy, even when there's nothing to be happy about. It means that you're happy when things go your way… and when things don't."

This, thought Maggie, would be a real challenge – until she tried it. When she lost a game of checkers to her brother, she decided to be as happy as if she'd won. What she found was that she was in charge of her own happiness; no one else. She decided then and there that it's better to be happy than not!

Ten requirements for being a great mermaid – Maggie had done them all. She vowed that she wouldn't stop, no matter what else she wanted to be. Being a great mermaid, she discovered, was about being the best that she could be. Now she knew how to do it!

That's how you make **<u>your</u>** world a better place – like Maggie, you become **Great**!

The end,
but not the end
of being your best.

At the end of this book you will find a Certificate of Merit that may be issued to any child who has fulfilled the requirements stated in the Certificate. This fine Certificate will easily fit into a 5"x7" frame, and happily suit any girl or boy who receives it!

Sally writes new books all the time. If you would like to be alerted when one of her new books becomes available or when one of her e-books is offered FREE on Amazon, sign up here: http://www.sallyhuss.com.

If you liked *The Official Mermaid Handbook,* please be kind enough to post a short review for it on Amazon. Thank you.

Here are a few Sally Huss books you might enjoy. They may be found on Amazon.

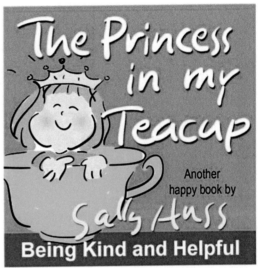

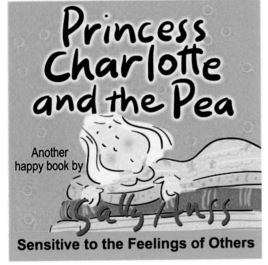

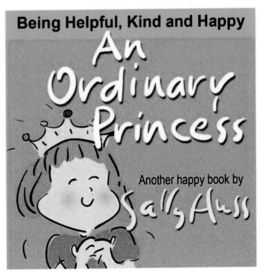

About the Author/Illustrator

Sally Huss

"Bright and happy," "light and whimsical" have been the catch phrases attached to the writings and art of Sally Huss for over 30 years. Sweet images dance across all of Sally's creations, whether in the form of children's books, paintings, wallpaper, ceramics, baby bibs, purses, clothing, or her King Features syndicated newspaper panel "Happy Musings."

Sally creates children's books to uplift the lives of children and hopes you will join her in this effort by helping spread her happy messages.

Sally is a graduate of USC with a degree in Fine Art and through the years has had 26 of her own licensed art galleries throughout the world.

This certificate may be cut out, framed, and presented to any child who has earned it.

Certificate of Merit

_____
(Name)

The child named above is awarded this
Certificate of Merit for:

*Striving to be the best that she or he can be
*Being a role model for others
*Showing respect for authority

Presented by: _____

Date: _____

Made in the USA
San Bernardino, CA
28 July 2018